Clinton Scollard

A boy's book of rhyme

Clinton Scollard

A boy's book of rhyme

ISBN/EAN: 9783337264871

Printed in Europe, USA, Canada, Australia, Japan

Cover: Foto ©Andreas Hilbeck / pixelio.de

More available books at **www.hansebooks.com**

A BOY'S BOOK OF RHYME

A BOY'S
BOOK OF RHYME

BY

Clinton Scollard

SICVT LILIVM
INTER SPINAS

BOSTON
COPELAND AND DAY
MDCCCXCVI

TO

ALL BOYS — YOUNG AND OLD

THE BOY

IN tasktime or in playtime,
  Or duty-bound or free,
From Maytime round to Maytime
  How wholly blithe is he !

Alert, with faun-like graces,
  His laughter mocks the rills ;
He brings from woodsy places
  The freshness of the hills.

His round cheeks' peachy flushes
  Are smothered half with tan,
His whistle 's like the thrush's,
  This foster-child of Pan.

He needs no necromancy
  His future to unfold ;
His forward flights of fancy
  Are bright with rainbow-gold.

His is life's truest treasure,
  The heritage of joy ;
Ah, who shall match or measure
  The warm heart of a boy !

Contents

For Any Boy

For Any Boy's Sister

VACATION-TIME

A BOY'S BOOK OF RHYME

VACATION–TIME

ALL the world is set to rhyme
Now it is vacation-time,
And a swelling flood of joy
Brims the heart of every boy.
No more rote and no more rule,
No more staying after school
When the dreamy brain forgets
Tiresome tasks the master sets ;
Nothing but to play and play
Through an endless holiday.

Morn or afternoon, may all
Swing the bat and catch the ball ;
Nimble-footed, race and run
Through the meadows in the sun,
Chasing wingèd scraps of light,
Butterflies in darting flight ;
Or where willows lean and look
Down at others in the brook,
Frolic loud the stream within,
Every arm a splashing fin.

Where the thorny thickets bar,
There the sweetest berries are ;
Where the shady banks make dim
Pebbly pools, the shy trout swim ;
Where the boughs are mossiest,
Builds the humming-bird a nest ; —
These are haunts the rover seeks,
Touch of tan upon his cheeks,
And within his heart the joy
Known to no one but a boy.

All the world is set to rhyme
Now it is vacation-time !

A BOY SPEAKS

THE POP-CORN MAN

THERE'S a queer little man lives down the
    street
Where two of the broadest highways meet,
In a queer little house that's half of it glass,
With windows open to all who pass,
And a low little roof that's nearly flat,
And a chimney as black as Papa's best hat.
Oh, the house is built on this funny plan
Because it's the home of the pop-corn man!

How does he sleep, if he sleeps at all?
He must roll up like a rubber ball,
Or like a squirrel, and store himself
All huddly-cuddly under the shelf.
If he wanted to stretch he'd scarce have space
In his bare little, spare little, square little place.
He seems like a rat cooped up in a can,
This brisk little, frisk little pop-corn man!

I know he's wise by the way he looks,
For he's just like the men I've seen in books,
With his hair worn off, and his squinty eyes,
And his wrinkles, too, — oh, I know he's wise!
And then just think of the way he makes
The corn all jump into snowy flakes,
With a "pop! pop! pop!" in his covered pan,
This queer little, dear little pop-corn man!

GOING TO SEA

I USED to say, " When I 'm a man,
   A jolly sailor I will be ;
I 'll have my own boat, if I can ;
   At least I know I 'll go to sea.''

And often to Papa I cried,
   Playing at ship with plank or pail,
" If this were but the ocean wide,
   Oh, how I 'd sail and sail and sail ! "

But now no more of boats for me !
   I 've had another better plan
Since Papa let me go to sea
   With Ben, the big brown sailor-man.

At first I thought it very nice ;
   You should have heard me laugh and shout ;
But when we tipped so once or twice
   I felt all turning inside out.

I 'd rather be our nursemaid, Ann,
   Who has to hear the baby bawl,
Than be a wretched sailor-man,
   And have no inside left at all !

FISHING

ONCE I went to fish with Phil,
   Up beside the old red mill,
Where the perch and pickerel
In their water-houses dwell.

6

I crawled out upon a log, —
Thought I'd sit there like a frog ;
But it acted just as mean
As a pony when it's "green,"
For it "bucked," and I fell right
In, and yelled with all my might.

Came a man a-running down,
Bushy-bearded, big and brown,
Leaned, and grabbed my roundabout
By the belt, and pulled me out,
Dripping, — wetter than a pike,
Shivery and "sousled-like."

Then he stood and slapped his knee,
Laughed, and shouted, "*Sakes o' me !
Queerest fish I ever see !*"

THE LITTLE BROWN WREN

THERE'S a little brown wren that has built
in our tree,
And she's scarcely as big as a big bumble-bee ;
She has hollowed a house in the heart of a limb,
And made the walls tidy and made the floor trim
With the down of the crow's-foot, with tow, and
with straw,
The cosiest dwelling that ever you saw.

This little brown wren has the brightest of eyes,
And a foot of a very diminutive size ;

The Little Her tail is as trig as the sail of a ship ;
Brown She 's demure, though she walks with a hop and
Wren.   a skip ;
And her voice — but a flute were more fit than
    a pen
To tell of the voice of the little brown wren.

One morning Sir Sparrow came sauntering by,
And cast on the wren's house an envious eye ;
With a strut of bravado and toss of his head,
" I 'll put in my claim here," the bold fellow
    said ;
So straightway he mounted on impudent wing,
And entered the door without pausing to ring.

An instant — and swiftly that feathery knight,
All towsled and tumbled, in terror took flight,
While there by the door on her favorite perch,
As neat as a lady just starting for church,
With this song on her lips, " *He will not call
    again
Unless he is asked*," sat the little brown wren.

THE SEARCH

I HAVE wandered long and far
Under sun and under star,
Up and down and to and fro,
Through the grass and through the snow,
Seeking for the secret dell
Where the happy fairies dwell.

8

Often those I met would say,
"You must search beyond the day;"
If a hill my steps defied,
I must "look the other side;"
If a stream ran swift before,
I must "try the further shore."

On I sped; 't was still the same,
And I never nearer came.
Ne'er I saw a guide-post stand
Pointing thus: ☞ To FAIRY LAND.
Although many seemed to know,
None the hidden way would show.

I believe it 's all a joke,
And there are no fairy-folk!

LITTLE MR. BY-AND-BY

LITTLE Mr. By-and-By,
You will mark him by his cry,
And the way he loiters when
Called again and yet again,
Glum if he must leave his play,
Though all time be holiday.

Little Mr. By-and-By,
Eyes cast down and mouth awry!
In the mountains of the moon
He is known as Pretty Soon;
And he 's cousin to Don't Care,
As no doubt you 're well aware.

Little Mr. By-and-By
Always has a fretful " Why ? "
When he 's asked to come or go,
Like his sister — Susan Slow.
Hope we 'll never — you nor I —
Be like Mr. By-and-By!

DUCKS

WHEN first the grass grows green in spring,
And from bare boughs the robins sing,
Before the orioles come back,
I hear the ducks go, " *Quack! quack! quack!* "

They paddle round and dive and float
Just where I like to sail my boat,
And when I run, from school set free,
They make such funny eyes at me.

They never cry, nor fuss, nor fret,
About the springtime rain and wet,
And have no need of sheltering roofs
Because they all wear " waterproofs."

THE YOUNG CRUSOE

NOW that the sweet flowers sleep
Where the snow is drifted deep,
And the chill winds roar and flout
So I may not play without,
In an ancient rocking-chair
O'er fanciful seas I fare,

And gleefully rise and dip
With the waves in my mimic ship,
Till my bark is wrecked on the strand
Of a lonely ocean land.

And then, like a workman skilled,
Out of books a hut I build
In the nook behind the couch,
Where I lurk with gun and pouch,
That no hungry savage there
May surprise me unaware.
If I spy my playmate Jim
Out I rush and capture him,
Overjoyed in heart to find
A Friday to suit my mind.

All around our isle we stray
And hunt through the golden day;
But when day's bright eye is shut
Then we seek my sheltered hut,
And sleep with our guns in hand
Until morning greets the land.
And at last from the lonely shore,
Just as Crusoe did of yore,
I sail o'er the windy main,
And arrive at home again.

THE GHOST

ONE summer day not long ago,
'T was in vacation-time I know,
We took our dinners, Jack and I, —
Some sugar-cookies and some pie, —
And with our hickory crossbows stout
We bravely for the woods set out.
The sun was hot.   Jack's face was red
As any turkey-gobbler's head,
And he said mine was like a piece
Of flannel with a coat of grease.
But we both laughed, and didn't care,
And let the wind blow through our hair,
And gave a shout, and ran until
We reached the bottom of the hill,
Just where the trees begin to throw
Their shadows on the grass below ;
And there we played at Indian ; then
We ate awhile, and played again.

And by and by a path we found
That through the forest wound and wound.
Jack said it was an Indian trail,
But I said " *Cows !* "   Then Jack grew pale,
Got awful mad, and wouldn't budge
Until I 'd hollered " pshaw ! " and " fudge ! "
A dozen times or so ; and then
We wandered on and on again,
Till suddenly a flash of light
Before us gleamed on something white,

And we both felt cold shivers run
Clear down our spines.   It wasn't fun !
" A ghost !" I cried.   The wind swept by ;
We thought we heard a mournful sigh,
And fled as though, with wild appeals,
A score of ghosts were at our heels.

But courage soon returned, and Jack
Declared aloud, " I 'm going back !"
So back we crept, still half afraid,
Through strips of shine and plots of shade,
Until before us suddenly
There stood, as plain as plain could be,
Our dreadful ghost — *a white birch tree !*

THE ARCHER

WHEN May has come, and all around
The dandelions dot the ground,
Then out into the woods I go,
And take my arrows and my bow.

Of hickory my bow is made,
Deep in a darksome forest glade
Cut from a sapling slim and tall,
And feathered are my arrows all.

And sometimes I am Robin Hood,
That olden archer brave and good ;
And sometimes I 'm an Indian sly,
Who waits to shoot the passers-by.

So up and down the woods I roam
Till sunset bids me hurry home
Before the pathway through the glen
Is peopled by the shadow-men.

And when at night my bow, unstrung,
Is close beside my quiver hung,
To bed I slip and slumber well,
And dream that I am William Tell.

HI-SPY

OH, when Bob and I
And Frank and Fred play Hi-Spy,
Round and round the barn we run,
Laugh and shout, — it's such fun !
In and out and up and down, —
Just the best old barn in town !
That's when Bob and I
And Frank and Fred play Hi-Spy !

From a corner in the mow
To our glossy bossy-cow
There's a chute to slide the hay
Where I hide myself away ;
Wondering where I can be,
How they hunt and hunt for me !
That's when Bob and I
And Frank and Fred play Hi-Spy !

14

Loud I call, and off they go,
Thinking I am far below ;
Then I cry again, and now
They declare I 'm in the mow,
And yet where they can't see,
So at last I 'm "in free ;"
That's when Bob and I
And Frank and Fred play Hi-Spy !

THE DRUMMER

THIS morning, when I went to play
Along the shady orchard way,
I heard a merry rat-tat-too
In branches where the breezes blew ;
But long in vain I tried to see
That tiny drummer in the tree.

At last I saw his speckled coat,
The sleek black velvet round his throat,
And perched upon his cunning head
A tufted little cap of red.
I cried to him : "Where come you from ?
And why do you so loudly drum ?"

He perked his head and looked at me,
But not an answering word said he.
Then in a moment from my sight
He darted like a ray of light.

Were I a drummer, I 'd not run
Unless I saw a big, big gun.

15

THE HAY–MOW

WHENE'ER I rise at morning-song,
    And see great cloud-banks black and long,
And hear the drum-sticks of the rain
Beat softly on the window-pane,
I know at ball I may not play,
Nor wander down the meadow-way
Where vines with juicy rubies grow,
And like white wheels the daisies blow.

But when my study-task is done,
Out to the hay-mow I may run,
And climb upon the rafters high
Where round the nesting swallows fly,
And twitter in their silly fear
Because they think a robber near ;
To be a robber's not my plan,
But play that I'm a diver-man.

The hills of hay, these are my sea,
And seem like waves far under me ;
Down, down I plunge with merry vim,
Then swiftly to the shore I swim,
And climb once more, and leap again
Into the middle of the main ;
It's so much fun, that if I can
Some day I'll *be* a diver-man !

FRAIDIE-CAT

I SHAN'T tell you what's his name :
When we want to play a game,
Always thinks that he'll be hurt,
Soil his jacket in the dirt,
Tear his trousers, spoil his hat, —
Fraidie-Cat! Fraidie-Cat!

Nothing of the boy in him !
"Dasn't" try to learn to swim ;
Says a cow 'll hook ; if she
Looks at him he 'll climb a tree.
"Scart" to death at bee or bat, —
Fraidie-Cat! Fraidie-Cat!

Claims the're ghosts all snowy white
Wandering around at night
In the attic : wouldn't go
There for anything, I know.
B'lieve he 'd run if you said "scat !"
Fraidie-Cat! Fraidie-Cat!

AN ARABIAN NIGHT

THE broad land glows with bright July,
And often when the day-beams fly,
And all the golden stars look glad,
Recalling tales of old Bagdad,
I softly stroll through garden-glooms
Amid the fragrant summer blooms,

An Arabian Night. And dream that I am wandering down
The byways of that orient town.

My Tigris is a stream that flows
'Twixt bowers where blooms the crimson rose ;
My boats are bubbles frail that glide
Serenely down the starlit tide ;
The nightingale that trills for me
Is robin in the apple-tree ;
The low wind-flutings from the firs
Are strains of harps and dulcimers.

The shrubs that bend in breezes bland
Are slaves that bow at my command ;
The arbor arched with tangled vine —
This is my pillared palace fine ;
The sentinels who guard the wall
Are tiger-lilies slim and tall ;
And over all I reign supreme,
The Caliph of my orient dream.

THE SAILOR

BEYOND the lawn, below the hill,
Runs, rippling by, a merry rill
That sings to me the sweetest tunes
Through all the summer afternoons,
For there I go to sail my boat
Till evening shadows round me float.

The stream I launch my craft upon
Is both my Rhine and Amazon,
And so I journey quite at will
In Germany or in Brazil ;
And oh, the scenes that form and shift
As down the dancing tide I drift !

Now castle towers frown over me,
Now monkeys leap from tree to tree ;
Now crags uprise on either side,
Now forest jungles billow wide ;
And ever do the cries prevail
Of those who set or furl the sail.

But by and by, my journeys from,
Into the quiet port I come ;
Then, like a hardy sailor-man,
I eat of dinner all I can ;
And when the night grows dark and deep,
I sail across the seas of sleep.

THE FAIRY PREACHER

I HEARD wind-elves in frolic pass
    As down the orchard path I strode,
And saw, amid the swaying grass,
    The pulpit of the preacher toad.

Alas ! I never set my tread
    Within these aisles at dusk or dawn,
But that I found the preacher fled,
    And all the congregation gone.

Yet some day at the service-time
  I 'll catch the fairy pulpiteer ;
Then how the cricket-choir will chime !
  And what a sermon I shall hear !

THE CASTLE-BOY

IN Spain Papa says castles stand
  On every hill-top in the land ;
I do not know where Spain may be,
Except that it 's across the sea ;
But sometimes when in bed I lie,
And not a star is in the sky,
I wish, while " patter " falls the rain,
I were a castle-boy in Spain.

Oh, I 'd have every kind of toy
If I were but a castle-boy !
I 'd have a bicycle and gun,
A pony that could swiftly run,
A pretty boat to sail or row,
And if, in winter-time, the snow
Should fall, I 'd have the finest sled,
And it should be all painted red.

I 'd play and play the whole day through,
And have no work at all to do ;
I 'd have the nicest things to eat,
And love to give my friends a treat ;

I 'd like Papa be, if I could,
For he is always kind and good ;
I 'd never cry, I 'd not complain,
Were I a castle-boy in Spain.

WHISPERERS

WHENEVER I go up or down
Along the roadway into town,
I hear a busy whispering there
Among the trees high up in air.

It 's clear to one who 's not a fool
That trees have never been at school ;
And if you ask me why I know —
It is because they whisper so !

WILLIE I-WONT-PLAY

WILFUL Willie I-Wont-Play
Always wants to have his way ;
With him it is *I* or *me*
Whatsoe'er the sport may be,
Prisoner's-Goal or Pull-Away, —
Wilful Willie I-Wont-Play.

If another faster run,
Though the game be just begun,
Then he 'll pout and sulk and scowl,
Gloomy as a day-caught owl,
Spoil the whole glad holiday, —
Wilful Willie I-Wont-Play.

Where's the boy would be like him,
Stout of arm and strong of limb,
Hearty as a sailor, yet
Ever in a selfish pet?
Shame upon his head, I say, —
Wilful Willie I-Wont-Play!

THE SWING

OUT in the yard, beneath the trees,
Where blithely blows the autumn breeze,
And where betwixt the leaves on high
There glimmer little strips of sky,
My sturdy swing is hung, and there
I make swift voyages far in air.

Now up and down I gayly go
Upon my journeys to and fro.
Whene'er I rise, upon my sight
Dawn meadows bathed in golden light;
Whene'er I dip, my eye perceives
A rustling bower of yellowing leaves.

The birds around me chirp and sing
As merrily I swing and swing;
But soon the birds will all be gone,
And snow will lie along the lawn,
So if I tread, my steps will show
Like Crusoe's Friday's long ago.

When winter winds in chorus call,
I do not use my swing at all,
But patiently I try to wait
Until returning robins mate ;
And when they cry to greet the spring,
Oh, how I join them from my swing !

THE BONFIRE

SOMETIMES, if I 've been very good,
I may go out to play
When twilight hides the distant wood
    And dims the orchard way.

Then at my rousing rally call
    Come Arthur, Frank, and Phil ;
And toward the garden dash we all
    Swift down the grassy hill.

A store from every hollow nook
    Our basket big receives ;
And in the corner by the brook
    We pile the fallen leaves.

And then when we have heaped them high
    To meet our hearts' desire,
We kindle them with merry cry
    And dance around the fire.

The little stars look down and blink
    To see such sights again ;
I 'm very sure they all must think
    That we are Indian men.

ROBIN

IF I were Robin, I just know
I'd not stand there and shiver so,
I'd spread my wings and soar on high,
And southward would I swiftly fly ;
For in the happy south, I'm told,
There's neither snow nor bitter cold.

There would I find a spreading tree,
And, oh, how merry I would be !
What cheery songs I would repeat,
And what delicious fruits I'd eat !
See ! Robin's off.   Perhaps he heard.
How nice it is to be a bird !

THE SLED

ON Christmas morning near my bed
I found the very nicest sled.
Good Santa Claus ! how did he know
It was the thing I wanted so ?

Now every day when school is out,
And all the boys with laugh and shout
Go racing home, I scamper, too,
And get my sled so bright and new.

We climb the hill, we push, we start,
And then like arrows downward dart ;
Nor do we pause until we gain
The middle of the snowy plain.

Again and yet again we climb,
With happy ardor every time ;
And if into a drift we run,
We count it all the greater fun.

When evening comes and lights are lit,
Beside the cheery fire I sit,
And think, when I go up to bed,
I 'd like to take along my sled.

THE SNOW-FORT

BEYOND the garden and the rill
We race to reach the orchard hill ;
There, in the wintry sunlight clear,
A mighty fort we swiftly rear ;
We make the ramparts thick and stout
To keep the furious foemen out,
And plant upon the highest wall
A banner proudly over all.

To arms ! — the volleys whistle round,
Yet bravely do we stand our ground ;
And backward in defeat at last
The army of the foe is cast.
Again they charge on us, and now
They rush across the white hill's brow,
While we, alas, are put to flight
For lack of arms wherewith to fight !

And thus our mimic wars we wage,
And many enemies engage ;
We conquer now, and now we fly,
And ever shout our battle-cry.
When comes the evening, chill and damp,
We seek the warm and sheltered camp,
And through the night, in visions, we
March on and on to victory.

THE SNOW–MAN

WHILE showed the moon her silver cup,
   Out of the south the wind blew up ;
The prisoned brooklet heard the stir,
And with the dawn the woodpecker
Sent all the orchard arches through
His unexpected rat-tat-too,
And pale icicles, every one,
Shed tears because they saw the sun.

When I went out-of-doors to play
With Jack — for it was holiday —
I saw our cousin Ned, who ran
And called to us, "*Let 's build a man !*"
So near the birch-tree, white and slim,
We trod a big, round place for him,
And rolled great puffy snowballs that
Would make him very tall and fat.
We got fresh snow, and soft and white,
To put his joints together right ;

26

Some shiny bits of coal, and round,
To fix a buttoned coat we found ;
Potatoes were his mouth and eyes,
Astonishing in shape and size ;
A rosy apple was his nose,
And last, to crown his head, we chose
A barrel-hoop, all set about
With turkey feathers stiff and stout.

And then we shouted, every one,
" *Hurrah ! hurrah ! he 's done ! he 's done !* "

THE SNOW-HOUSE

ALL yesterday it snowed and snowed,
And all last night, until the road
Was whiter than the downy spread
Upon my cozy trundle-bed.
And once, before the daylight broke,
When from the land of dreams I woke,
I heard the poor wind whine and moan
Like Carlo when he 's left alone.
Then high above the fleecy plain
The red sun sprang, and shook his mane,
And every window seemed like cake
The busy city bakers make.
So I got all my warm wraps out,
And buttoned tight my roundabout,
And found my shovel in the shed,
And shouted loud and long to Ned,
Until he came with answering cries,
All bundled to the very eyes ;

Then down the orchard path we ran,
And Ned was rear and I was van.

With doleful wail the wind still blew,
And, oh, what drifts we floundered through !
The apples clinging to the bough
Were like big bursting puff-balls now ;
The brook was smothered ; not a note
Came gurgling from its merry throat,
And only cheery chickadee
Sang welcome from the cherry-tree.
Beside the fence was piled the snow
As high as pony's back, I know ;
And there we cleared a space before
A humpy drift, and made a door,
And hallway wide to light the gloom,
And then a great round sitting-room,
Whose roof was set with shining things
That looked as bright as Mamma's rings.
We had to creep along the hall,
But didn't have to here at all ;
And snug within our house of snow
We played that we were Esquimaux.

FOR ANY BOY

THE CROW

OHO ! oho ! Sir Sable-Plume,
With your glossy coat,
And your grating note,
And your darkly mysterious air of gloom ;
Now that the north winds keenly blow,
And the valleys and hills are white with snow,
Why don't you wing
To the land of spring,
Away to the south, away, away,
From the cold and the ice and the wintry day ?

To a bird of brain
It ought to be plain
That it must be pleasanter far to caw
Where the warm sun shines
On the blossoming vines,
By the grassy banks of the Chickasaw,
Than here from the tops of the chilly pines.

And oh, to think of the orange-trees,
And the palms of the isles of the Caribbees !
And then how nice
To breathe the spice
That floats on every waft of the breeze !
Never a wind to chill you through,
And make you shiver and quiver and shake,
But skies of blue,

And silver dew,
And fruits as sweet as a frosted cake.

You prefer to stay !
Is that what you say ?
Well, crows and boys like to have their way.

A SPRING MEETING

(ROBIN TO WREN.)

HULLO, Bob Wren !
Are you back again ?
Glad to see you so well and so merry ;
Fear we 're here
Rather early this year !
Dear, but I wish I 'd a bite of a cherry !
Just ripe in the South,
Melt in your mouth.
Weren't you sorry to leave the sunny
Land of bloom, and of bees and honey ?

By and by here 't will be bright and jolly
With bud and blossom, but somehow now
The atmosphere seems melancholy,
For there 's not a leaf on a single bough ;
And the wind, oh, how it makes you shiver,
And long for the balmy air that blows
The reeds that quiver
Above some river
That warm in Floridian sunlight flows !

Have you any new songs to sing this season ?   *A Spring*
And do you know where you are going to stop ?   *Meeting.*
We 've taken rooms in the very top
Of " The Maple " — prices quite within reason.
You 've a flat near by that you 've leased till fall ?
How nice !   Then surely you 'll come and call.

THE LITTLE EGYPTIAN BOY

THE little Egyptian boy
    Has dusky cheeks of brown ;
He wears a long, long gown,
And a funny cap on his head,
That is tasselled and round and red ;
You hardly would suppose
That his shoes could pinch his toes,
For they 're anything but small,
And they have no heels at all.
He must be full of fun,
And his legs — how they *can* run !

   The little Egyptian boy
Has never seen the snow ;
Where the palms and fig-trees grow
It is summer the whole year through,
And the sky is blue — so blue !
A donkey is the toy
Of the little Egyptian boy,
And he often goes to ride
Where the clover-fields reach wide,
And he loves to race and shout
And frolic and romp about.

The little Egyptian boy
Sings queer, wild songs, and plays
In the very strangest ways ;
And he looks so grave and wise
Out of his big, black eyes !
But he does not dare to stray
Very far from his home away,
For he 'd come to the river Nile,
And a hungry crocodile
Would quickly go "snap ! snap !"
Oh, wouldn't that be a sorry hap
For the little Egyptian boy !

BOBOLINK

BOBOLINK —
He is here !
Spink-a-chink !
Hark ! how clear
Drops the note
From his throat,
Where he sways
On the sprays
Of the wheat
In the heat !
Bobolink,
Spink-a-chink !

Bobolink
Is a beau.
See him prink !
Watch him go

34

Through the air
To his fair !
Hear him sing
On the wing —
Sing his best
O'er her nest !
   " Bobolink,
   Spink-a-chink ! "

Bobolink,
   Linger long !
There 's a kink
   In your song
Like the joy
Of a boy
Left to run
In the sun —
Left to play
All the day.
   Bobolink,
   Spink-a-chink !

E PUSSY–CAT BIRD

TO–DAY when the sun shone just after the
   shower,
A song bubbled up from the lilac-tree bower
That changed of a sudden to quavers so queer,
For a moment I thought something wrong in my
   ear.
Then I called little Dempster, and asked if he
   heard.

35

"Oh, yes !" he replied; "it's the pussy-cat bird."

The pussy-cat bird has the blackest of bills,
With which she makes all of her trebles and trills :
She can mimic a robin, or sing like a wren,
And I truly believe she can cluck like a hen ;
And sometimes you dream that her song is a word,
Then quickly again — she's a pussy-cat bird !

The pussy-cat bird wears a gown like a nun,
But she's chirk as a squirrel, and chock-full of fun.
She lives in a house upon Evergreen lane, —
A snug little house, although modest and plain ;
And never a puss that was happier purred
Than the feathered and winged little pussy-cat
bird.

MADAM ROBIN'S AFTERNOON TEA

ONE afternoon
In the heart of June,
The very brightest, bluest weather,
Some of the song-birds came together.
They met at Madam Robin's, you see,
In the top of a breezy maple-tree,
For she'd asked them in to an "early tea."

All were dressed
In their very best ;
Mr. Jay wore an azure vest ;

36

Mistress Sparrow and Lady Wren,
The one in brown and the one in yellow,
Fluttered merrily in, and then
Came Sir Bobolink — jolly fellow !
Timid Miss Phœbe and pert Miss Thrush
Followed Lord Oriole, spick and sprightly ;
Next the Finches with rustle and rush,
And Parson Blackbird beaming brightly.

And there were others, a score —
Or more —
All in the very merriest mood, too ;
And there rose such a patter,
And clatter, and chatter,
That those not invited
Were soon quite affrighted,
For nobody knew what on earth was the matter,
Or what such a babel of talk could allude to.

But nothing alarming
Heard those overhead, so
They found it quite charming,
And each of them said so ;
For they'd all been south, and they hadn't met
Since the autumn-time with its chill and wet.

So this was all that the babel meant :
They were asking each other with rapt intent,
" Where and how was your winter spent ? "

THE RAG-MAN

O UT of the distance far and faint,
Up from the vale like a plover's plaint,
Nearing slowly until it seems
To die away like a call in dreams,
Swelling again to leap with a bound
To a whimsical crest like a wave of sound,
Now a quaver and now a quirk,
Now a twist like a vocal smirk,
            Comes the cry —
"Rags! O—h, rags! Any rags to buy?"

See him driving along the road,
Singing and shouting above his load !
A tawny, grizzly, odd little elf,
Just a bundle of rags himself ;
With eyes that sparkle under his lashes
Like living coals in the whitened ashes ;
Eager, alert, with his word of cheer
For his rag-like horse of the shaggy ear ;
            And still the cry —
"Rags! O—h, rags! Any rags to buy?"

On and on through the sun and rain,
Lifting ever his sole refrain,
Up and over the hills and down,
Courting the country-side and town,
Always chirk as a merry grig
Tuning under a lilac twig,
Always free as the wind to roam,

'The whole wide sweep of the land his home ;
      And ever the cry —
" *Rags !*   *O—h, rags !   Any rags to buy ?* "

BOLDIE DOG

A PATTER of feet at the door, and hark,
   The blithest, briskest, breeziest bark !
A head alert like a grenadier
When a sound suspicious greets his ear ;
A tail that swings like a soldier's sword
When he charges down on a hostile horde ;
Fleet as a faun over brake and bog,
That 's the way with the Boldie Dog !

Sinewy, supple, soft, and sleek,
With fur as smooth as a maiden's cheek,
And great, deep brooding eyes that show
How the happy dog-dreams come and go ;
In the gladdest, maddest plunge and play
He races and chases the livelong day,
Then lies at night like a very log,
That 's the way with the Boldie Dog !

He likes to rest his head on your hand
With a look that says — " You understand ; "
Or he loves to lead with bound and leap
Through forest paths where the ferns are deep ;
Always ready and ever true, —
A friend to the end whate'er you do ;
Frisk as a grig and chirk as a frog,
That 's the way with the Boldie Dog !

A BOY'S SONG IN SPRING

HURRAH, for the snow is over,
And the merry brook is free !
We 'll soon sip sweets from the clover
Along with the bumble-bee.

We 'll track the soaring swallow
As he eddies above the trees,
And follow him and follow,
And dream of the things he sees.

We 'll watch the insects springing
Till they seem like roguish elves,
And hark to the brown thrush singing
Till we want to sing ourselves.

Hurrah, for the snow is over !
And Winter, the poor old soul,
Has gone to play the rover
On the meadows of the pole.

THE SQUIRREL

NOW that russet leaves are tost
In the mornings keen with frost,
Now that nuts have burst the burr —
Chir-r-r ! Chir-r-r !

You may hear it,
Hark, how clear it
Rises from the elm and fir !

'T is the cheery squirrel's call,
Cold-defying voice of fall ;
List the merry chatterer!
    Chir-r-r! Chir-r-r!

He's not sober,
Though October
Is among the days that were.

FAIRY FOOD

SAID my blue-eyed cousin John,
  "What do fairies live upon?"
And he looked in eager wise
At me with his bright young eyes.

" Every morning-time," I said,
" They bake tiny loaves of bread ;
Cricket-steaks they often eat ;
And their drink is honey sweet
From the honeysuckle bell,
Or the crimson clover-cell ;
They have berry pie and tart
Flavored with a rose's heart ;
And a very favorite thing
Is a slice of beetle's wing."

" Pooh," cried John, " no wonder that
Fairies are not big or fat!"

GOSSIPS

DEEP in the woodland you will hear,
If you but lend attentive ear,
A murmurous talk from time to time,
And all the words will run to rhyme.
By light of sun and light of star,
The wind and trees the gossips are ;
In whispers to the questioning trees
The wandering wind tells all he sees,
For he can roam and roam and roam,
While all the trees must stay at home.

DON

OH, a dear little dog is Don,
With a dash of family pride !
As sleek as satin to look upon,
    Frisky and glow-worm-eyed.
He steps like a drummer-boy
    Perking his head up high,
And the cup of his pleasure brims to joy
    When Carroll comes with a cry :
        For it 's *"Rats!"* he says; *"Rats!
        Rats!"* he says :
        (Or it 's *" Cats!"* he says).
                That 's
                    When you should see Don.

He will play at hide-and-seek
    With the vim of a brisk north breeze,
Or he 'll crouch all quiet and meek
    At a touch on the ivory keys.

Cuddly and warm and round   *Don.*
    He will lie like a velvet ball,
But up he 'll leap with a bark and a bound
    At the sound of Carroll's call :
        For it 's *"Rats!"* he says; *"Rats!*
        Rats!" he says :
        (Or it 's *" Cats!"* he says).
                    That 's
                        When you should see Don.

RAIN

I T 'LL *rain! It 'll rain!*
  Says the peacock's shrill refrain,
Ere the heaven shows for sign
E'en a single leaden line.
See, a silvery shudder now
Runs along the poplar bough !
And recurrent ripples pass
O'er the reaches of the grass.
Low the swallows circle over
Rosy fields of scented clover ;
Willows whiten in the lane —
It 'll rain! It 'll rain!

It 'll rain! It 'll rain!
Watch the shifting weather-vane
Veering from its dreams of drouth
Toward the veiled and showery south !
Now the eye of day is hid
Underneath a lowering lid,

Rain.

And the heaven feels the lash
Of a goading lightning-flash.
Peals a bell with soft insistence
Clearly down the darkening distance,
And the peacock cries again —
It'll rain! It'll rain!

THE TRUMPETER

CAN you hear it? Hark, it rings!
Airiest of trumpetings;
Sounding through the sunny weather,
Calling wingèd things together
To a feast of honey, found
In deep goblets red and round.
Belted is the trumpeter
And he wears a gallant spur.
His array is freaked with gold,
And his buoyant air and bold
Is his knightly birthright. Oh,
See him puff his cheeks and blow!

What strange trumpeter is he, —
Do you ask? The honey-bee!
Where the climbing vines embower
Playing on a trumpet-flower.

IN THE AUGUST TWILIGHT

FROM the hillside wheat-fields brown
Blithely stride the gleaners down
Through the laneways where the lowing

44

Cattle greet them, homeward going ;
Sinewy muscles, bronze and bare,
Glints of sunset on their hair
That the zephyr from the croft
Touches with its fingers soft ;
Mellow murmurs from the flashing
Pebbly runnel, onward dashing ; —

*Purple shadows gently falling,
    And, in waving tree-tops hid,
Raucous voices calling, calling,
    " Katydid ! "*

Every grass blade by the road
Bends beneath its dusty load ;
Mullein, dock, and morning-glory,
All are clad in raiment hoary ;
In the skies a ghostly moon
Grows as dies the afternoon ;
From the marshes far below
Frogs their deep bass trumpets blow ;
Further than the eye can follow
Up the azure flits the swallow ; —

*Purple shadows gently falling,
    And, in waving tree-tops hid,
Strident voices calling, calling,
    " Katydid ! "*

THE WHISTLER

HE came up over the hill
In the flush of the early morn,
And he blew his whistle shrill
    Till the blackbirds down in the corn,
And the robins, all were still.

And the leaves began to lean,
    And the little blades of grass,
And the lily garden-queen,
    All eager to see him pass, —
He of the frolic mien.

They watched for his back-tossed hair,
    And his peachy lips a-purse,
And his tan cheeks full and fair,
    As he flung a flute-like verse
Into every nook of the air.

But never a trace could they find
    Of his form, though they knew him near ;
And their bright eyes were not blind.
    You will marvel not to hear
That the whistler was the wind.

THE DANCERS

RUSSET and ruddy and amber
    The cheeks of the dancers are ;
So light their feet they could clamber
    The stairway up to a star.

46

When you think they are standing steady, *The Dancers.*
  With never a dream of a swirl,
They break into boisterous eddy,
  And are off with a whisk and a whirl.

They meet in a march sedately,
  Then change to a trip or a trot ;
They leap from a minuet stately
  To the swing of a gay gavotte.

They perk into prim position ;
  They rally, retreat, advance ;
And the wind is the blithe musician
  That plays for the leaves to dance.

WHERE ARE THE FAIRIES GONE?

WHERE are the fairies gone,
  Now that the woods are brown,
And lace lies over the lawn
  As white as the thistledown ?

Did they rig them a ruddered barque,
  With sails of the golden leaves,
And venture upon the dark
  In the cool of the autumn eves ?

Did they follow the songbird's flight,
  Swiftly winging away
Out of the northern night
  Into the southern day ?

The queen, the court, and the king,
Mab and her Oberon, —
Will they come again in the spring ?
Where are the fairies gone ?

BY THE YULE-LOG

A RHYME, and a light and lithe one,
That sways like a supple vine ;
A song, and a bright and blithe one,
A-flood with the Christmas-shine.

A catch, and a clear and glad one,
Like the brook-note in the spring ;
A stave, and a gay and mad one,
That shall make the rafters ring.

Then it's cheer, my masters merry,
And cheer, my bonny maids, O !
Our song's for the holly berry,
Our kiss for the mistletoe !

FOR ANY BOY'S SISTER

DOWN IN THE STRAWBERRY BED

JAYS in the orchard are screaming, and hark,
Down in the pasture the blithe meadow-lark
Floods all the air with melodious notes !
Robins and sparrows are straining their throats.
" Dorothy ! Dorothy ! " — out of the hall
Echoes the sound of the musical call ;
Song birds are silent a moment, then sweet,
" Dorothy ! " all of them seem to repeat.

Where is the truant ?   No answer is heard,
Save the clear trill of each jubilant bird ;
Dawn-damask roses have naught to unfold,
Sweet with the dew and the morning's bright
    gold.
" Dorothy ! Dorothy ! " — still no reply,
None from the arbor or hedgerow anigh ;
None from the orchard where grasses are deep,
" Dorothy ! " — surely she must be asleep !

Rover has seen her ; his eyes never fail ;
Watch how he sabres the air with his tail !
Follow him ! follow him !   Where has he gone ?
Out toward the garden and over the lawn.
" Dorothy ! Dorothy ! " — plaintive and low,
Up from the paths where the hollyhocks grow,
Comes the soft voice with a tremor of dread,
" *Dorofy 's down in 'e stwawbewy bed !* "

Curls in a tangle and frock all awry,
Bonnet, a beam from the gold in the sky,

Eyes with a sparkle of mirth brimming o'er,
Lap filled with ruby fruit red to the core.
Dorothy ! Dorothy ! rogue that thou art !
Who at thee, sweet one, to scold has a heart ?
Apron and fingers and cheeks stained with red,
Dorothy down in the strawberry bed !

LADY HOLLYHOCK

SLENDER Lady Hollyhock,
In your green and crimson frock,
Many are your lovers gay
Dancing down the garden way.
But beware how you believe
What the merry gallants say,
Lest the fickle ones deceive !

Blithe Sir Butterfly may hover,
Honey-Bee his heart declare,
Humming-Bird his love discover,
One and all their fealty swear, —
Every ready vow 's a snare !

Blithe Sir Butterfly makes bold
To entreat the Marigold ;
And with ardor Honey-Bee
Sues the delicate Sweet-Pea ;
While the truant Humming-Bird
Many a bloom woos warily
With his false but winning word.

So, my slender little lady,
    By their favors be not won !
But in quiet cool and shady,
    Looking out upon the sun,
    Dwell contented like a nun.

*Lady
Hollyhock.*

THE FIRST EDITION OF THIS BOOK CONSISTS
OF FIVE HUNDRED COPIES PRINTED DURING
OCTOBER 1896 BY THE ROCKWELL AND
CHURCHILL PRESS OF BOSTON